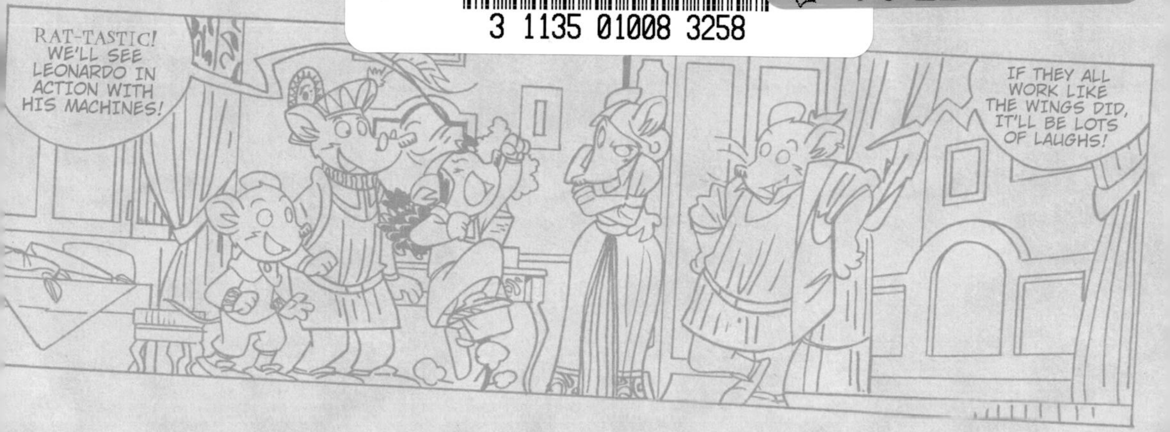
RAT-TASTIC! WE'LL SEE LEONARDO IN ACTION WITH HIS MACHINES!
IF THEY ALL WORK LIKE THE WINGS DID, IT'LL BE LOTS OF LAUGHS!

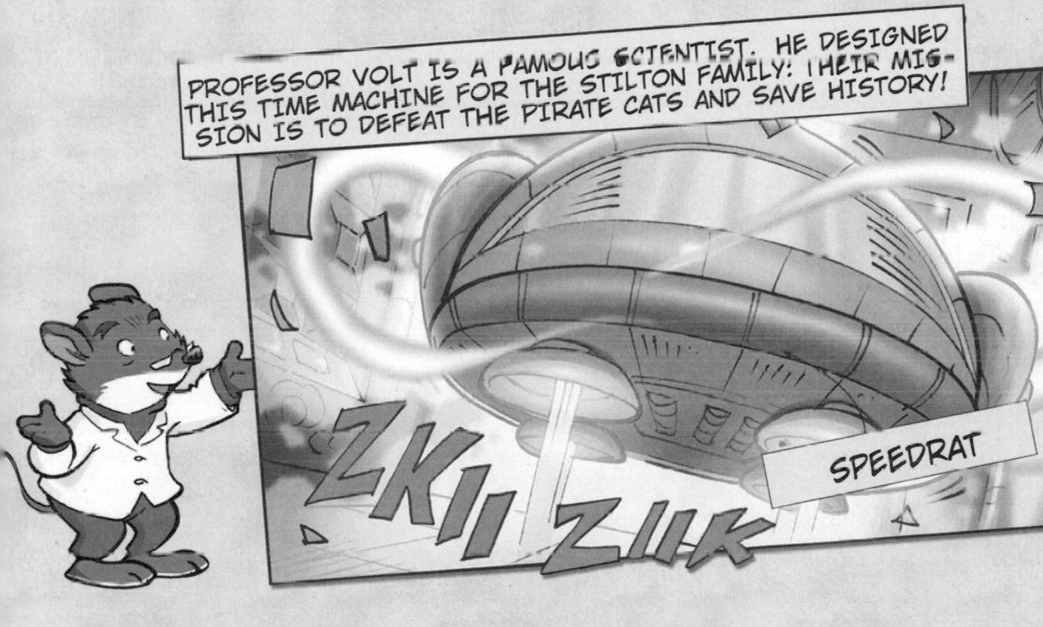
PROFESSOR VOLT IS A FAMOUS SCIENTIST. HE DESIGNED THIS TIME MACHINE FOR THE STILTON FAMILY: THEIR MISSION IS TO DEFEAT THE PIRATE CATS AND SAVE HISTORY!
ZKII ZIIK
SPEEDRAT

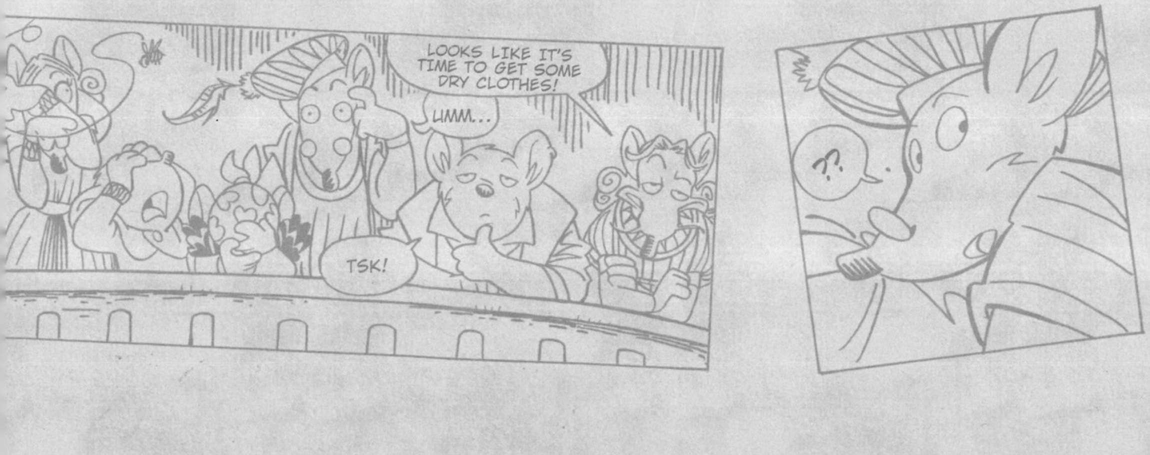
LOOKS LIKE IT'S TIME TO GET SOME DRY CLOTHES!
UMM...
TSK!
?!

Geronimo Stilton

WHO STOLE THE MONA LISA?

PAPERCUTZ™

GRAPHIC NOVELS AVAILABLE FROM

PAPERCUTZ™

All-new, full-color Graphic Novel
Geronimo Stilton
THE DISCOVERY OF AMERICA
PAPERCUTZ

All-new, full-color Graphic Novel
Geronimo Stilton
THE SECRET OF THE SPHINX
PAPERCUTZ

All-new, full-color Graphic Novel
Geronimo Stilton
THE COLISEUM CON
PAPERCUTZ

All-new, full-color Graphic Novel
Geronimo Stilton
FOLLOWING THE TRAIL OF MARCO POLO
PAPERCUTZ

Graphic Novel #1
"The Discovery of America"

Graphic Novel #2
"The Secret of the Sphinx"

Graphic Novel #3
"The Coliseum Con"

Graphic Novel #4
"Following the Trail of Marco Polo"

Graphic Novel #5
"The Great Ice Age"

Graphic Novel #6
"Who Stole The Mona Lisa?"

COMING SOON:
Graphic Novel #7
"Dinosaurs in Action"

Geronimo Stilton graphic novels are
available in hardcover for $9.99 each.
Please add $4.00 for postage and
handling for the first book,
add $1.00 for each additional book.
Please make check payable to
NBM Publishing.
Send to:
Papercutz, 40 Exchange Place,
Suite 1308,
New York, NY 10005

All-new, full-color Graphic Novel
Geronimo Stilton
THE GREAT ICE AGE
PAPERCUTZ

All-new, full-color Graphic Novel
Geronimo Stilton
WHO STOLE THE MONA LISA?
PAPERCUTZ

All-new, full-color Graphic Nove
Geronimo Stilton
DINOSAURS IN ACTION

www.papercutz.com

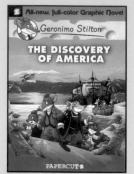

Geronimo Stilton

WHO STOLE THE MONA LISA?

By Geronimo Stilton

PAPERCUTZ™
New York

WHO STOLE THE MONA LISA?
© EDIZIONI PIEMME 2009 S.p.A.
Tiziano 32, 20145,
Milan, Italy
Geronimo Stilton names, characters and related indicia are copyright, trademark and
exclusive license of Atlantyca S.p.A.
All rights reserved.
The moral right of the author has been asserted.

Text by Geronimo Stilton
Editorial coordination by Patrizia Puricelli
Original editing by Daniela Finistauri
Script by Demetrio Bargellini
Artistic coordination by Roberta Bianchi
Artistic assistance by Tommaso Valsecchi
Graphic Project by Michela Battaglin
Graphicss by Marta Lorini
Cover art and color by Flavio Ferron
Interior illustrations by Giuseppe Facciotto and color by Christian Aliprande
With the collaboration of Ambrogio M. Piazzoni.

© 2010 – for this work in English language by Papercutz.

Original title: Geronimo Stilton Chi Ha Rubato la Gioconda?

Translation by: Nanette McGuinness

www.geronimostilton.com

Lettering and Production by Ortho
Michael Petranek – Associate Editor
Jim Salicrup
Editor-in-Chief

ISBN: 978-1-59707-221-2

Printed in China.

August 2010 by WKT Co. LTD.
3/F Phase 1 Leader Industrial Centre
188 Texaco Road, Tsuen Wan, N.T.
Hong Kong

Distributed by Macmillan.
First Printing

WHO STOLE THE MONA LISA?

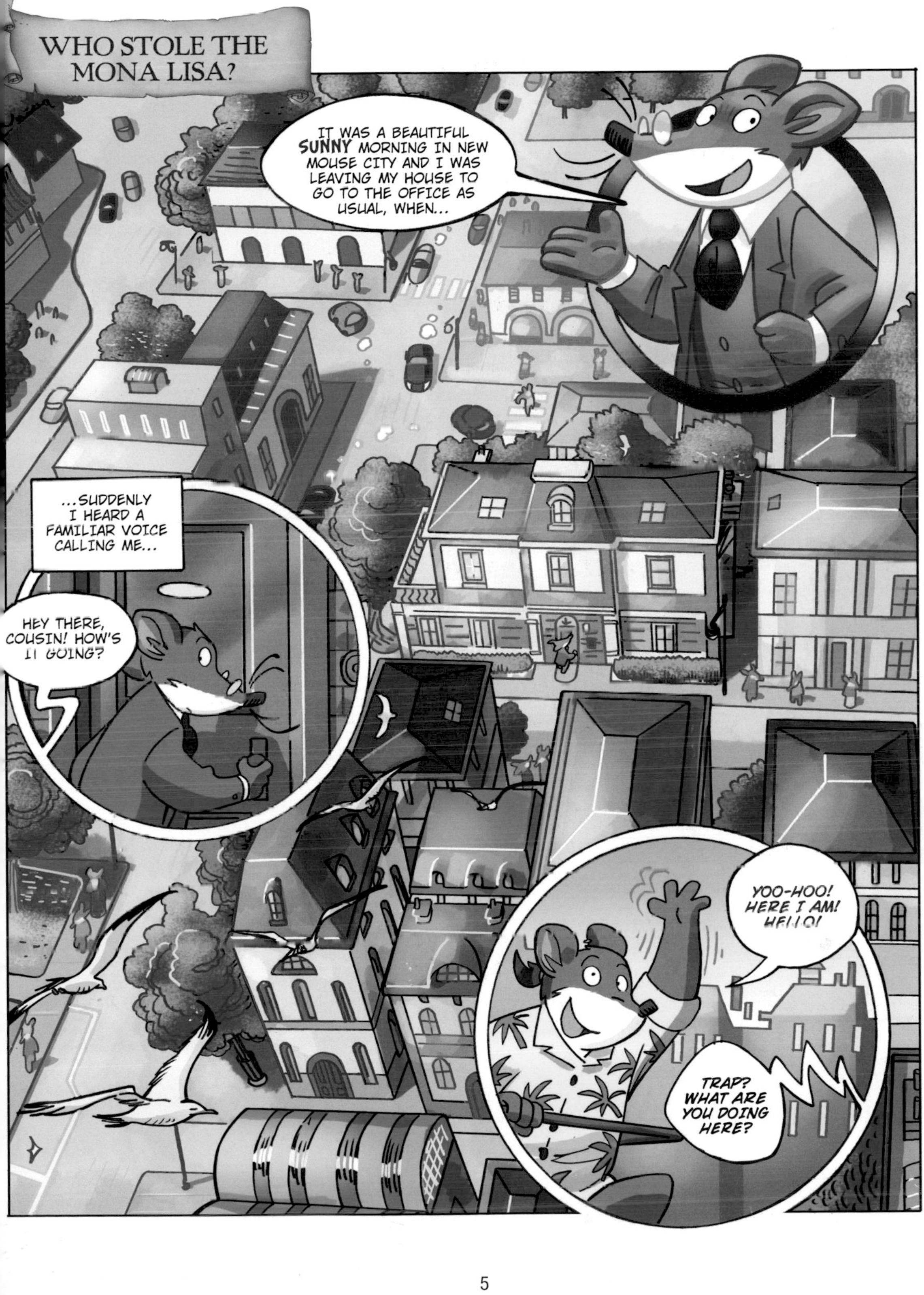

IT WAS A BEAUTIFUL SUNNY MORNING IN NEW MOUSE CITY AND I WAS LEAVING MY HOUSE TO GO TO THE OFFICE AS USUAL, WHEN...
...SUDDENLY I HEARD A FAMILIAR VOICE CALLING ME...
HEY THERE, COUSIN! HOW'S IT GOING?
YOO-HOO! HERE I AM! HELLO!
TRAP? WHAT ARE YOU DOING HERE?

HOP ON BOARD! I'LL TAKE YOU TO YOUR OFFICE IN MY RICKSHAW!

YOUR RICKSHAW?!? UMM...OKAY!

OH, SORRY! I FORGOT TO INTRODUCE MYSELF... MY NAME IS STILTON, *Geronimo Stilton!* AND I EDIT THE RODENT'S GAZETTE.

GO SLOWLY! YOU KNOW I GET CARSICK!

THEN **YOU** DRIVE. THAT WAY YOU WON'T WORRY!

WHAT?!? ME? BUT... BUT...WHY?

COME ON, GERONIMO, DON'T BE ALL SAD AND WHINY! IF YOU DRIVE, YOU'LL FEEL JUST FINE!

BUT... BUT... I DON'T KNOW IF I CAN DO IT!

I GRANT YOU THE HONOR AND AWE OF DRIVING MY BRAND NEW RICKSHAW... THE ONLY ONE I HAVE!

COME ON, WE'RE WASTING TIME. LET'S GO!

A LITTLE LATER, ON THE STREETS OF NEW MOUSE CITY...

YOU'RE A VERY GOOD DRIVER, COUSIN!

OH, COULD YOU STOP AT THE BAKERY AND LEND ME SOME DOUGH FOR SOME CAKE?

>SIGH!<

MEANWHILE IN CATBURG, THE CAPITAL OF CAT ISLAND...

ANY **NEWS**, TERSILLA?

NONE YET, DADDY DEAR!

THE EXPERTS CONFIRM THAT THIS PARCHMENT FOUND IN THE GALLEON DATES BACK TO 1500...

...BUT IT'S WRITTEN IN A MYSTERIOUS CODE THEY CAN'T DECIPHER!

IT MUST HAVE DIRECTIONS FOR FINDING A CAT-TASTIC TREASURE!

WE'LL PROCEED WITH OUR PLAN! GET READY TO LEAVE FOR MOUSE ISLAND!

MOUSE ISLAND?!? WHAT'RE WE GOING TO DO THERE?

SILENCE, YOU PAIN IN THE TAIL*!

MEOOOW!

*PAIN IN THE NECK

MEOW DOWN,* BONZO! CATARDONE WILL EXPLAIN EVERYTHING TO YOU ALONG THE WAY!

FOR NOW, WE'VE FIGURED OUT THAT SOMETHING'S WRITTEN ON THE PARCHMENT AND WE'RE GOING TO TEACH GERONIMO STILTON A LOVELY LESSON...HEE, HEE, HEE!

*CALM DOWN

THAT NIGHT, IN NEW MOUSE CITY...

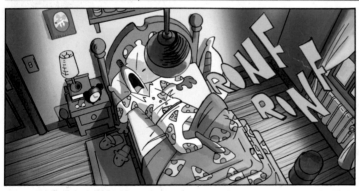

RONF RONF

RONF RONF

Rrinnggg... rringgg...

...rrinnggg... attention, call for Geronimo Stilton... rrinngg...

...rrinnggg... Geronimo, it's Ampy Volt. Do you hear me?

8

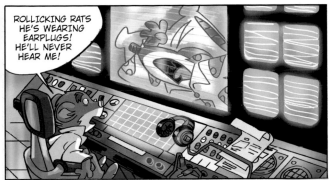

ROLLICKING RATS HE'S WEARING EARPLUGS! HE'LL NEVER HEAR ME!

I'LL HAVE TO RESORT TO THE EMERGENCY ALARM I HID UNDER HIS BED!

Click

SQUEEEAK!

SWEEEEIIIING

CRASH

MOLDY MOZZARELLA! WHAT HAPPENED?

Hello, GERONIMO, DO YOU HEAR ME?

?!?

PROF. VOLT... IS THAT YOU?

IT IS, INDEED! YOU AND YOUR FRIENDS MUST COME OVER TO MY CAMPER-LABORATORY IN FRONT OF THE *RODENT'S GAZETTE.* HURRY!

9

HISTORY IS IN DANGER AGAIN!

>GULP!< I'LL GET DRESSED AND BE RIGHT THERE, PROFESSOR!

I MUST LET THE OTHERS KNOW... I HOPE I CAN FIND A TAXI RIGHT AWAY!

HEY THERE, COUSIN. NEED A LIFT?

OH, NO!

A LITTLE LATER, ALONG WITH THEA, TRAP, BEN-JAMIN, AND PANDORA, I ARRIVED AT VOLT'S LAB...

HERE WE ARE, PROFESSOR... >PANT, PANT<...

?!?

GERONIMO, IS EVERYTHING ALL RIGHT?

Y-YES...

SORRY TO BOTHER YOU, BUT IT'S AN EMERGENCY!

IS IT THE PIRATE CATS AGAIN, PROFESSOR?

UNFORTUN-ATELY, YES, PANDORA: THEY'RE TRAVELING INTO THE PAST AGAIN WITH THEIR TIME MACHINE!

THOSE CRUMMY CATS WANT TO CHANGE HISTORY TO THEIR BENEFIT!

ARE YOU OKAY, THEA? YOU'RE AS WHITE AS A SLICE OF MOZZARELLA!

M-ME? YES... YES!

IT'S JUST... CAN'T SEEM TO DIGEST THE TALEGGIO CHEESE FONDUE I HAD FOR DINNER.

WHERE ARE THE PIRATE CATS HEADED THIS TIME?

TO AMBOISE, IN FRANCE, IN THE YEAR 1517!

FRANCE

OWES ITS NAME TO THE ANCIENT GERMANIC POPULATION, THE FRANKS, WHO CONQUERED THE REGION IN THE FOURTH CENTURY AD. THEIR FIRST KING, CLOVIS (481-511), CAME FROM THE MEROVINGIAN LINE. AFTER THE FRENCH REVOLUTION, IN 1789, FRANCE WAS PROCLAIMED A REPUBLIC, BUT UNDER NAPOLEON BONAPARTE, IT BECAME AN EMPIRE (1804) AFTER VARIOUS EVENTS, FRANCE WAS ONCE AGAIN PROCLAIMED A REPUBLIC IN 1871, WITH PARIS AS ITS CAPITAL.

B-B-BUT... HOW DO YOU KNOW THIS?

?!?

POOR THEA, SHE REALLY MUST HAVE EATEN TOO MUCH!

I'M SURPRISED BY YOUR QUESTION, THEA! BY NOW YOU SHOULD KNOW ABOUT THE TEMPOGRAPH, THE DEVICE I USE TO MONITOR THE COURSE OF HISTORY!

UM... RIGHT, OF COURSE... THE TEMPOGRAPH... HOW SILLY OF ME!

THAT'S NOT IT! THAT'S JUST AN OLD CUCKOO CLOCK!

KOO-KOO

?!?

THIS IS THE TEMPOGRAPH!

YOU MUST HAVE EATEN SOMETHING REALLY GREASY, LITTLE COUSIN!

GETTING BACK TO THE PIRATE CATS, I'M AFRAID THEIR TARGET MAY BE THE FAMOUS SCIENTIST AND ARTIST **LEONARDO DA VINCI**. AT THAT TIME HE LIVED IN THE FRENCH TOWN OF AMBOISE, IN THE CASTLE OF CLOUX, AS A GUEST OF FRANCIS I, THE KING OF FRANCE!

LEONARDO DA VINCI (1452-1519) PAINTER, SCULPTOR, ARCHITECT, SCIENTIST, AND INVENTOR LEONARDO DA VINCI IS CONSIDERED ONE OF THE GREATEST GENIUSES WHO EVER LIVED. HE WAS BORN IN VINCI, A VILLAGE NEAR FLORENCE, IN ITALY. HIS MOST FAMOUS WORKS OF ART INCLUDE "THE LAST SUPPER" WHICH HE PAINTED IN THE CHURCH OF SANTA MARIA DELLA GRAZIE IN MILAN AND THE PAINTING, "LA GIOCONDA," ALSO KNOWN AS THE "MONA LISA," WHICH IS KEPT TODAY AT THE LOUVRE MUSEUM IN PARIS.

UMM... >GULP< ARE YOU SAYING...?

THAT THEY WANT TO STEAL A *PAINTBRUSH AND PAINTS?*

MAYBE THEY WANT TO STEAL THE MONA LISA!

THE ONLY WAY TO FIND OUT IS FOR US TO GO THE SIXTEENTH CENTURY, TO AMBOISE, TOO.

A LITTLE LATER, WE WERE IN THE SPEEDRAT, READY TO GO...

ONBOARD ARE CLOTHES FROM THE PERIOD AND EARPLUGS THAT WILL LET YOU SPEAK THE LOCAL LANGUAGE!

THANKS, PROFESSOR! DON'T WORRY, WE'LL STOP THE PIRATE CATS!

DO YOU FEEL LIKE DRIVING, THEA?

OF COURSE, I FEEL LIKE IT! WHAT A QUESTION!

LET'S SEE... HOW DO I TURN THIS THING ON?

HMMM... LET'S TRY THIS BUTTON!

CLICK

?!?

SPLASH

HMPH...

THAT'S THE BUTTON FOR THE EJECTION SEATS!

MAYBE YOU SHOULD DRIVE, TRAP!

MEANWHILE, THE PIRATE CATS HAD LANDED NEAR AMBOISE IN THE YEAR 1517 IN THE MIDDLE OF THE RENAISSANCE...

THERE WE GO, THE CATJET IS COMPLETELY **CAMOUFLAGED!**

DID YOU REMEMBER TO BRING THE **PAINT** CANS?

THE RENAISSANCE

THE PERIOD IN HISTORY FROM THE END OF THE 1300S AND THE MIDDLE OF THE 1500S IS CALLED THE RENAISSANCE. THE NAME COMES FROM THE FACT THAT AFTER THE MIDDLE AGES, WHICH WERE CHARACTERIZED BY POVERTY AND LITTLE ECONOMIC GROWTH, EUROPE EXPERIENCED A PERIOD OF QUICK DEVELOPMENT, ACTUALLY A "REBIRTH," BOTH ECONOMICALLY, ARTISTICALLY, AND CULTURALLY. "RENAISSANCE" MEANS "REBIRTH" IN FRENCH.

YES, YES... EVEN THOUGH I'M NOT SURE WHAT WE'RE USING THEM FOR!

I'LL TELL YOU LATER! IS THE REST OF THE PLAN CLEAR?

HMM... SURE! WE HAVE TO KIDNAP LEONARDO DA VINCI AND BRING HIM WITH US TO CATBURG!

EXACTLY! ACCORDING TO TERSILLA, HE'S THE ONLY ONE WHO CAN DECODE THE MYSTERIOUS PARCHMENT!

LEONARDO WILL BE ABLE TO TRANSLATE THE CODE. THEN WE CAN ALSO ASK HIM TO INVENT A RAT-CATCHING MACHINE!

BUT HOW ARE WE GOING TO KIDNAP HIM?

WE'LL PRETEND TO BE TWO FRENCH **PAINTERS** WHO WANT TO BECOME HIS PUPILS!

PAINTING IN THE RENAISSANCE

DURING THIS PERIOD, PAINTERS PERFECTED THE USE OF PERSPECTIVE TO PORTRAY THE DEPTH AND PROPORTIONS OF OBJECTS JUST AS WE SEE THEM (FOR EXAMPLE, BY DRAWING OBJECTS THAT ARE FAR AWAY SMALLER). PAINTERS ALSO PAID A GREAT DEAL OF ATTENTION TO STUDYING THE BODY AND ITS MOVEMENT ANATOMICALLY.

AND WHEN WILL TERSILLA GET HERE?

SHE'LL CATCH UP WITH US AT THE RIGHT TIME! HER JOB IS VITAL FOR OUR **PLAN** TO SUCCEED!

COME ON! LET'S PUT ON OUR MOUSE MASKS AND CLOTHING FROM THE PERIOD.

AFTER A FEW MINUTES...

LEONARDO WILL NEVER SUSPECT WE'RE CATS!

NOW WE'RE JUST MISSING THE FINAL TOUCH!

UMM... AND THAT WOULD BE?

PAINTERS ALWAYS HAVE PAINT ALL OVER THEM!

SPLAFF

MEOW!

NOW YOU REALLY LOOK LIKE A PAINTER! SHALL I GIVE YOU A COAT OF YELLOW PAINT, TOO?

FIRST LET ME GIVE YOU A HAND!

>GULP!<

HOW *DARE YOU!?!?* GRRR... I'LL... I'LL... ATOMIZE* YOU!

*DESTROY YOU!

A LITTLE LATER, THE CATS ARRIVED AT THE CASTLE OF CLOUX.

THE CASTLE OF CLOUX WAS LOCATED ONLY 500 METERS FROM THE ROYAL CASTLE OF AMBOISE. AT THE REQUEST OF KING FRANCIS I OF FRANCE, LEONARDO DA VINCI STAYED THERE FROM 1517-1519, THE YEAR HE DIED. TODAY THE CASTLE IS CALLED CLOS LUCE AND HOUSES A MUSEUM DEDICATED TO THE GREAT ARTIST.

16

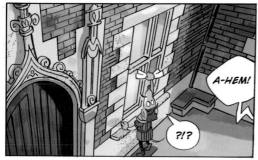

A-HEM!

?!?

MELTING CAMEMBERT!

GOOD DAY! IS THIS THE HOME OF MASTER LEONARDO?

WH-WH-WHO ARE YOU? WH-WH-WHAT DO YOU WANT?

MY NAME IS CATARD OF CAT AND THIS IS BONZETON LEBONZE. WE'RE PAINTERS!

PAINTERS?!?

SURE, DON'T YOU SEE HOW WE'RE COVERED WITH PAINT?

FORGIVE ME, I THOUGHT YOU WERE VAGRANTS! I'M BATTISTA, MASTER LEONARDO'S SERVANT!

WELL, BATTISTA, COULD YOU TELL THE MASTER THAT WE'D LIKE TO MEET HIM?

I'M SORRY, BUT HE'S BUSY WITH AN EXPERIMENT AND CANNOT BE DISTURBED!

LEONARDO'S MACHINES

BESIDES BEING A GREAT ARTIST, LEONARDO WAS ALSO A CLEVER INVENTOR AND SCIENTIST. HE DEVISED MACHINES THAT CAN BE CONSIDERED THE "ANCESTORS" OF MANY MODERN INVENTIONS, SUCH AS CARS, BICYCLES, MOTORBOATS, AND EVEN A HELICOPTER. HE WAS THE FIRST TO ENVISION DEVICES THAT HUMANS WOULD ONE DAY USE TO FLY WITH.

NOW WHAT'RE WE GOING TO DO?

HMPH...WILL HE BE BUSY FOR A WHILE?

IT DEPENDS ON WHETHER HE IS ABLE TO STOP!

TO STOP?!?

GET OUT OF THE WAY, OVER THERE! MAKE WAY! MAKE WAY!

UH?

OUT OF THE WAY! I'VE LOST CONTROL OF THE MACHINE!

WROOOOMM

RUN FOR YOUR LIFE!

HELPPPPP!

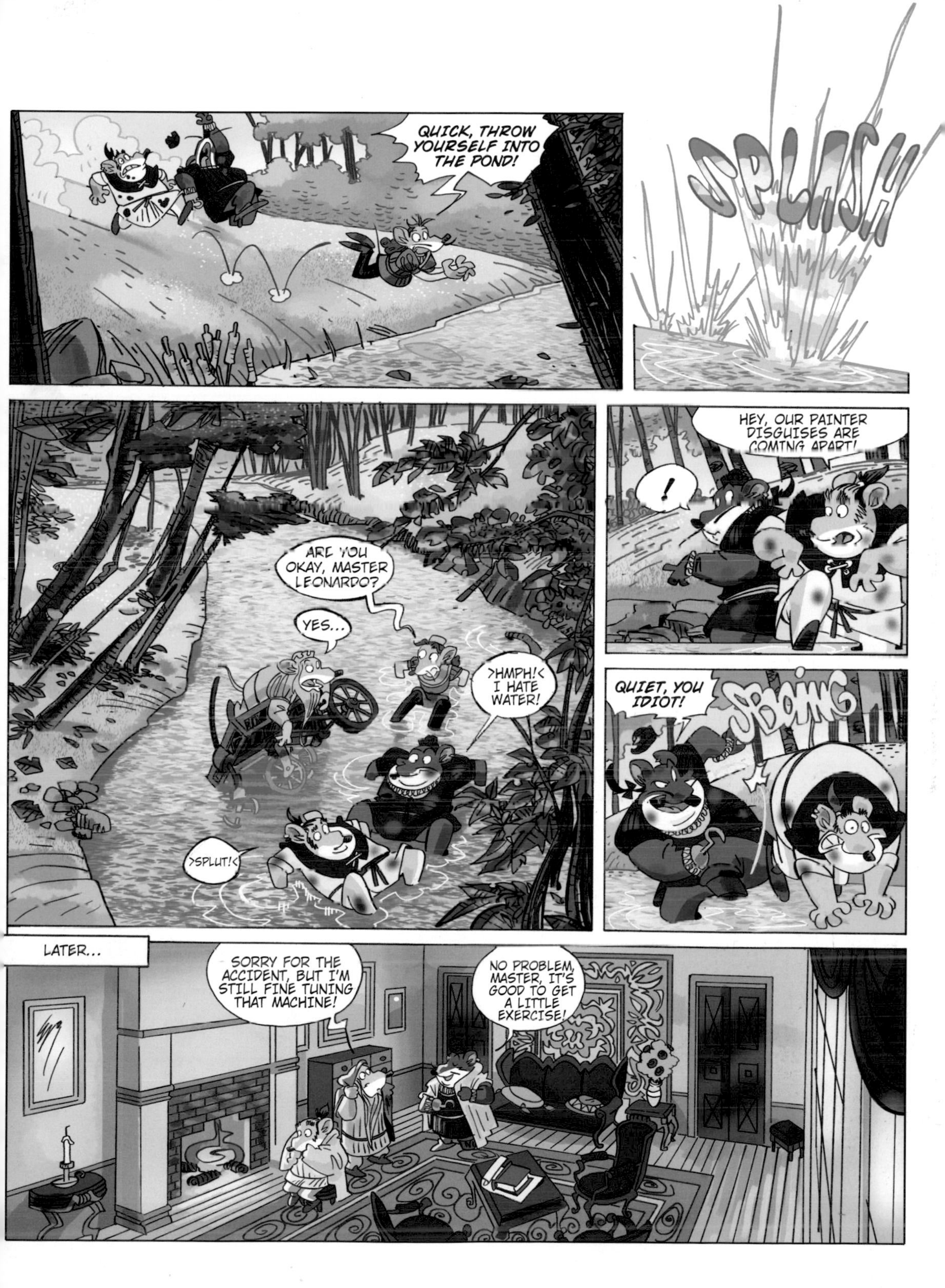

QUICK, THROW YOURSELF INTO THE POND!
SPLASH
ARE YOU OKAY, MASTER LEONARDO?
YES...
>HMPH!< I HATE WATER!
>SPLUT!<
HEY, OUR PAINTER DISGUISES ARE COMING APART!
!
QUIET, YOU IDIOT!
SBOING
LATER...
SORRY FOR THE ACCIDENT, BUT I'M STILL FINE TUNING THAT MACHINE!
NO PROBLEM, MASTER, IT'S GOOD TO GET A LITTLE EXERCISE!

CLOCKWORK CAR

EQUIPPED WITH THREE WHEELS AND A STEERING WHEEL, THIS CAR IS ALSO KNOWN AS "LEONARDO DA VINCI'S CAR." IT WAS BUILT WITH SPRINGS AND GEARS THAT ENABLED THE CAR TO MOVE.

BATTISTA MENTIONED TO ME THAT YOU'RE ALSO **PAINTERS!**

ACTUALLY WE'RE JUST HUMBLE BEGINNERS!

WE WANT YOU TO TEACH US ALL THE SECRETS OF PAINTING!

I'M SORRY TO DISAPPOINT YOU, BUT I SELDOM DO ANY PAINTING NOWADAYS!

I DO NEED ASSISTANTS, HOWEVER, TO TEST-DRIVE MY MACHINES!

UH-OH!

UM... >GULP!<... WE'D BE **HONORED!**

BUT I WARN YOU: IT'S VERY DANGEROUS WORK!

WE CA... >AHEM<, RODENTS ARE AFRAID OF NOTHING!

THEN YOU CAN HELP ME WITH MY EXPERIMENTS AND I'LL GIVE YOU PAINTING LESSONS IN EXCHANGE!

IT'S A DEAL!

HMM... I PREDICT A *SEA* OF TROUBLES!

20

IN THE MEANTIME, MY FRIENDS AND I HAD ARRIVED NEAR AMBOISE.

NICE LANDING, TRAP!

THANKS, COUSIN! YOU'RE TOO KIND!

ACTUALLY... I WAS BEING SARCASTIC!

HEY, WE'RE SAFE AND SOUND, RIGHT?

YES, BUT WE'RE UP A TREE!

SO? WE WON'T EVEN HAVE TO HIDE THE SPEEDRAT!

BUT I'M AFRAID OF HEIGHTS! HOW AM I SUPPOSED TO GET DOWN?

YOU DON'T WANT ME TO CARRY YOU DOWN ON MY BACK, DO YOU, COUSIN?

WHILE YOU KEEP TALKING, I'M *LEAVING...*

?!?

WOW! WHAT A **RAT-TASTIC** LEAP!

>GULP!<

A FEW MINUTES LATER, AFTER STARTING TO GET READY...

DON'T FORGET TO PUT ON PROFESSOR VOLT'S EARPHONES!

ARE WE GOING STRAIGHT TO THE CASTLE OF CLOUX, UNCLE GERONIMO?

YES, LEONARDO IS OUR ONLY **CLUE!**

SO LET'S GET GOING!

HOW EXCITING: WE'RE IN THE MIDDLE OF THE RENAISSANCE!

AND SOON WE'LL EVEN MEET LEONARDO DA VINCI!

THIS IS THE CASTLE OF AMBOISE! CLOUX IS A LITTLE FARTHER ON!

AMBOISE CASTLE

WAS BUILT IN THE 13TH CENTURY ON A BLUFF OVERLOOKING THE LOIRE RIVER IN CENTRAL FRANCE. IN THE FOLLOWING CENTURIES, LARGE GARDENS AND WIDE TERRACES WERE CREATED HANGING OVER THE RIVER. KING FRANCIS I OF FRANCE USED AMBOISE CASTLE AS HIS HOME WHEN HE STAYED IN THE LOIRE VALLEY.

SOON, WE REACHED THE CASTLE OF CLOUX...

STRANGE, NO ONE SEEMS TO BE AROUND...

I'LL TRY KNOCKING ON THE DOOR!

BUT... WE CAN'T DISTURB LEONARDO WITHOUT A REASON!

GERONIMO, YOU TOLD US LEONARDO WAS OUR ONLY CLUE!

23

YES, BUT, WHAT WILL WE SAY TO LEONARDO?

I DON'T KNOW, BUT WE HAVE TO START LOOKING FOR THE CATS SOMEWHERE!

AHOY DOWN THERE, WATCH OUT BELOW!

?!?

SBAM

SQUEAK!

WINGS

AMONG HIS DIFFERENT INVENTIONS, LEONARDO DESIGNED WINGS FOR FLYING THAT WERE LIKE THE WINGS OF A BAT AND COULD BE ATTACHED TO A FLYING MACHINE. THE WINGS WERE MADE OF FABRIC STRETCHED OVER A WOOD AND BAMBOO FRAME.

CRISPY CRACKERS! GERONIMO STILTON!

POOR UNCLE! HE TOOK A SOLID HIT!

OWIEOWIE! OWIEOWIE!

WAS SOMEBODY HURT?

NO, NOT EVEN A SCRATCH!

>GROAN!<

EXCUSE ME... WOULD YOU MIND TELLING ME WHO YOU ARE?

MY NAME IS STIL...THAT IS, STILTONEAUX, GEROME STILTONEAUX!

AND THIS IS MY NEPHEW BELMOUSE, HIS FRIEND PANDORETTE, MY SISTER THEA AND MY COUSIN TRAPO FALON.

WE ARE MERCHANTS FROM MARSEILLE... AND WOULD LIKE TO BUY ONE OF YOUR WORKS OF ART!

MARSEILLE? MERCHANTS???

WELCOME! BATTISTA WILL GET A ROOM READY FOR YOU IMMEDIATELY!

YOU'RE VERY KIND!

GOOD DAY, MASTER LEONARDO, I SEE YOU HAVE MANY VISITORS TODAY!

WHAT?

AH, GOOD DAY, YOUR MAJESTY!

THAT MUST BE KING FRANCIS I OF FRANCE!

THEN WE HAVE TO BOW, PANDORA!

FRANCIS I (1494-1547)

WAS BORN IN COGNAC, FRANCE IN 1494. IN 1514 HE WAS GRANTED THE TITLE OF DUKE OF VALOIS AND MARRIED CLAUDIA, DAUGHTER OF KING LOUIS XII OF FRANCE, BECOMING HIS LEGITIMATE SUCCESSOR. ONCE HE ASCENDED TO THE THRONE, FRANCIS I FOCUSED PRIMARILY ON FOREIGN POLICY, BUT HE NEVER LET THAT END HIS PASSION FOR THE ARTS AND LITERATURE. MANY ITALIAN POETS AND ARTISTS BESIDES LEONARDO LIVED AT THE COURT OF THE KING.

ARE THESE RODENTS YOUR NEW ASSISTANTS?

ONLY CATARD AND BONZETON... THE OTHERS ARE MERCHANTS WHO WANT TO BUY MY PAINTINGS!

WHAT? YOU'RE NOT THINKING OF SELLING THE PAINTINGS YOU PROMISED TO ME, RIGHT?

I WOULD NEVER DARE OFFEND MY PATRON LIKE THAT!

I SHOULD CERTAINLY HOPE NOT!

YOU KNOW THEY'RE PREPARED TO PAY ANY PRICE JUST TO HAVE THE PAINTING OF THE **SMILING LADY!**

HUH?

I CAME SPECIFICALLY TO ADMIRE IT!

I WOULD BE HAPPY TO ACCOMPANY YOU TO MY STUDIO, SIRE! AND WITH YOUR PERMISSION, I WOULD ALSO LIKE TO SHOW THE PAINTING TO MY NEW FRIENDS!

SO BE IT! BUT DON'T FORGET THAT YOU PROMISED IT TO ME!

La Gioconda

LA GIOCONDA, ALSO CALLED THE "MONA LISA," IS LEONARDO DA VINCI'S MOST FAMOUS PAINTING. HE PAINTED IT BETWEEN 1503 AND 1506 ON A PLANK OF POPLAR WOOD, USING OIL PAINTS. WE STILL AREN'T CERTAIN ABOUT THE IDENTITY OF THE WOMAN HE PAINTED. ACCORDING TO SOME SCHOLARS, SHE WAS MONA LISA GHERARDINI, THE WIFE OF FRANCESCO BARTOLOMEO DEL GIOCONDO (WHOSE NAME WAS USED FOR THE PAINTING). THE PAINTING WAS MADE IN FLORENCE AND AFTERWARDS LEONARDO TOOK IT WITH HIM WHEREVER HE LIVED.

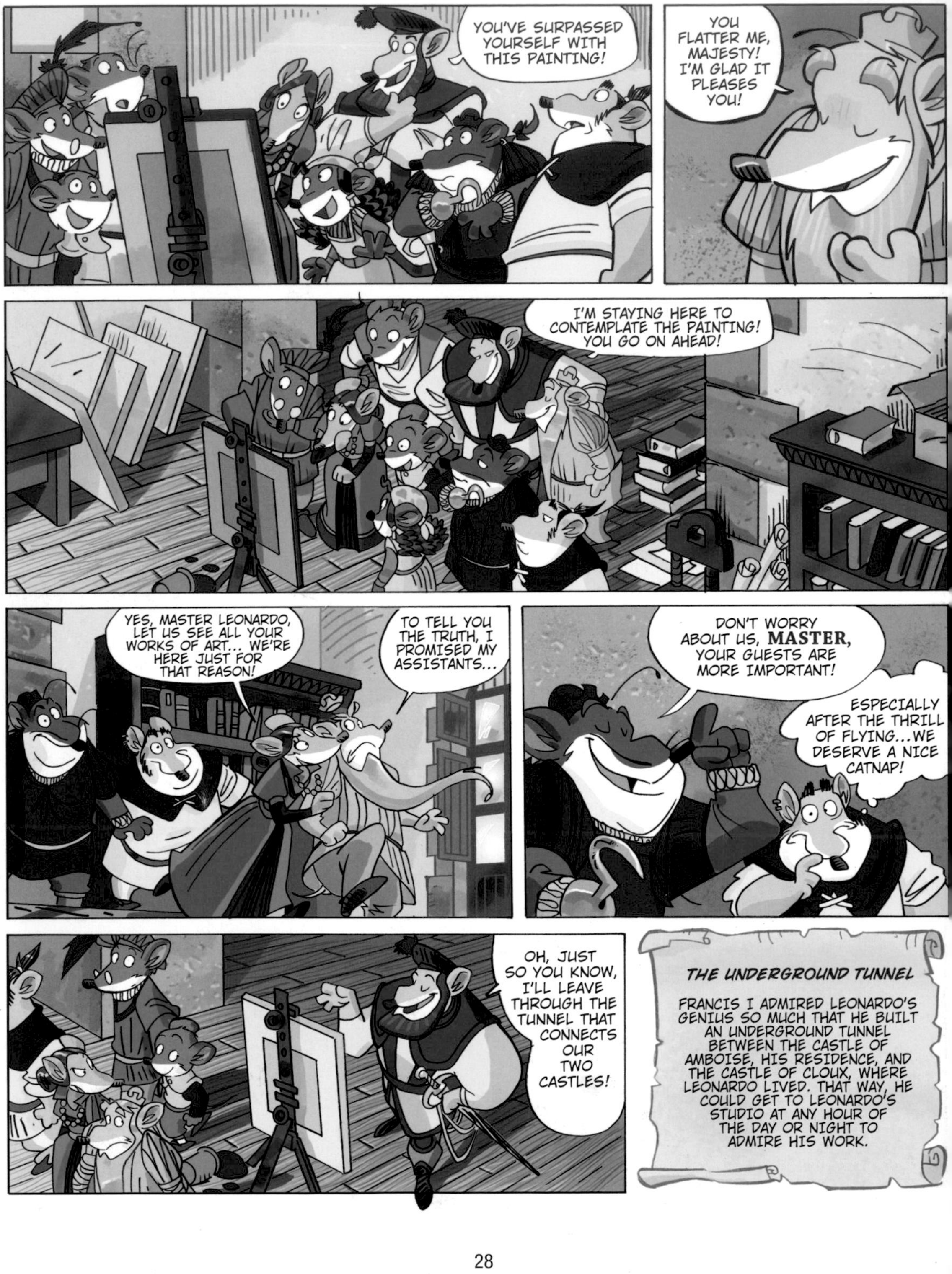
YOU'VE SURPASSED YOURSELF WITH THIS PAINTING!
YOU FLATTER ME, MAJESTY! I'M GLAD IT PLEASES YOU!
I'M STAYING HERE TO CONTEMPLATE THE PAINTING! YOU GO ON AHEAD!
YES, MASTER LEONARDO, LET US SEE ALL YOUR WORKS OF ART... WE'RE HERE JUST FOR THAT REASON!
TO TELL YOU THE TRUTH, I PROMISED MY ASSISTANTS...
DON'T WORRY ABOUT US, **MASTER**, YOUR GUESTS ARE MORE IMPORTANT!
ESPECIALLY AFTER THE THRILL OF FLYING...WE DESERVE A NICE CATNAP!
OH, JUST SO YOU KNOW, I'LL LEAVE THROUGH THE TUNNEL THAT CONNECTS OUR TWO CASTLES!
THE UNDERGROUND TUNNEL
FRANCIS I ADMIRED LEONARDO'S GENIUS SO MUCH THAT HE BUILT AN UNDERGROUND TUNNEL BETWEEN THE CASTLE OF AMBOISE, HIS RESIDENCE, AND THE CASTLE OF CLOUX, WHERE LEONARDO LIVED. THAT WAY, HE COULD GET TO LEONARDO'S STUDIO AT ANY HOUR OF THE DAY OR NIGHT TO ADMIRE HIS WORK.

LATER, AFTER SHOWING US ALL HIS WORK, LEONARDO WENT BACK TO HIS EXPERIMENTS...

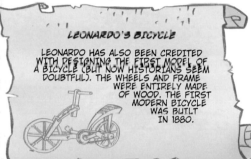

LEONARDO'S BICYCLE

LEONARDO HAS ALSO BEEN CREDITED WITH DESIGNING THE FIRST MODEL OF A BICYCLE (BUT NOW HISTORIANS SEEM DOUBTFUL). THE WHEELS AND FRAME WERE ENTIRELY MADE OF WOOD. THE FIRST MODERN BICYCLE WAS BUILT IN 1880.

...WHILE WE GOT TOGETHER IN THE ROOM THEY'D GIVEN I KAP AND ME.

SO... DID YOU NOTICE ANYTHING *SUSPICIOUS?*

YES, SOMETHING IS STRANGE ABOUT HIS TWO ASSISTANTS.

IN FACT, THEY'RE A LITTLE WEIRD!

BUT THAT'S NOT PROOF THEY'RE CATS.

WHAT IF LEONARDO ISN'T THE CAT'S REAL **TARGET?**

RIGHT... MAYBE THEY'RE MORE INTERESTED IN THE KING!

TRAP'S NOT ALTOGETHER WRONG! MAYBE FRANCIS I COULD BE THEIR TARGET!

MAYBE THEY WANT TO KICK HIM OFF THE FRENCH THRONE.

RIGHT, BUT...WHY DIDN'T THEY GO STRAIGHT TO PARIS?

WE DON'T KNOW... FOR NOW, IT'S BETTER IF WE STAY AT CLOUX AND KEEP AN EYE ON LEONARDO'S ASSISTANTS AND SERVANT!

RAT-TASTIC! WE'LL SEE LEONARDO IN ACTION WITH HIS MACHINES!

IF THEY ALL WORK LIKE THE WINGS DID, IT'LL BE LOTS OF LAUGHS!

AT MIDNIGHT...

30

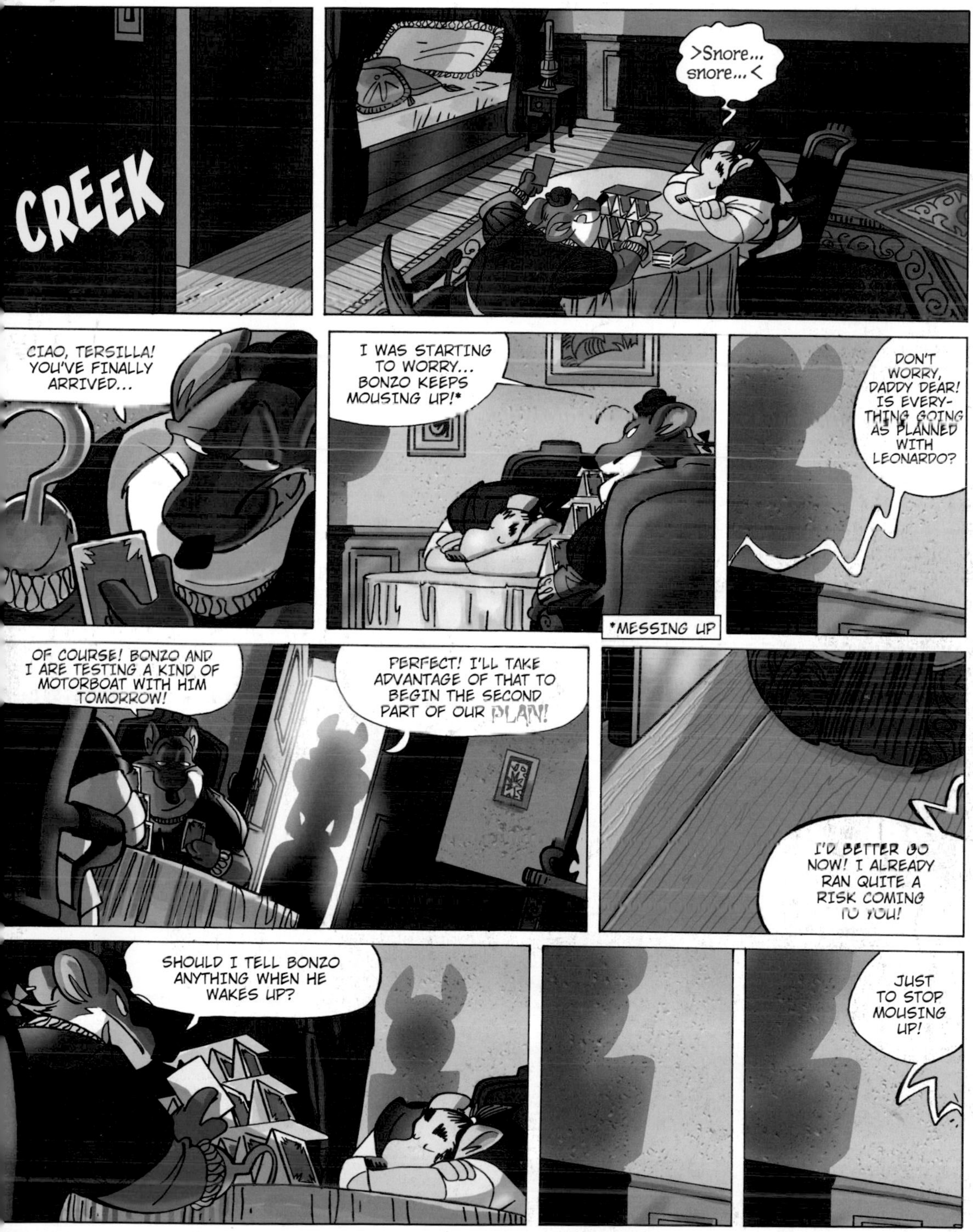
CREEK
>Snore... snore...<
CIAO, TERSILLA! YOU'VE FINALLY ARRIVED...
I WAS STARTING TO WORRY... BONZO KEEPS MOUSING UP!*
*MESSING UP
DON'T WORRY, DADDY DEAR! IS EVERYTHING GOING AS PLANNED WITH LEONARDO?
OF COURSE! BONZO AND I ARE TESTING A KIND OF MOTORBOAT WITH HIM TOMORROW!
PERFECT! I'LL TAKE ADVANTAGE OF THAT TO BEGIN THE SECOND PART OF OUR PLAN!
I'D BETTER GO NOW! I ALREADY RAN QUITE A RISK COMING TO YOU!
SHOULD I TELL BONZO ANYTHING WHEN HE WAKES UP?
JUST TO STOP MOUSING UP!

THE NEXT MORNING, LEONARDO SUMMONED US TO THE BANKS OF THE CHANNEL TO WATCH HIM LAUNCH HIS "PADDLE BOAT."

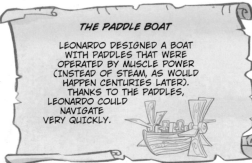

THE PADDLE BOAT

LEONARDO DESIGNED A BOAT WITH PADDLES THAT WERE OPERATED BY MUSCLE POWER (INSTEAD OF STEAM, AS WOULD HAPPEN CENTURIES LATER). THANKS TO THE PADDLES, LEONARDO COULD NAVIGATE VERY QUICKLY.

WHEN I SHOW YOU HOW THIS BOAT WORKS, YOU'LL BE SPEECHLESS!

UMM... MASTER LEONARDO... I HAVE TO TELL YOU SOMETHING...

LATER, BONZETON! I'M TALKING!

MASTER LEONARDO, IT'S IMPORTANT!

HMPH! TELL ME WHAT YOU WANT?

THE BOAT IS SINKING!

FRANTIC FRESH FRESCOES!

HURRY! START PADDLING!

32

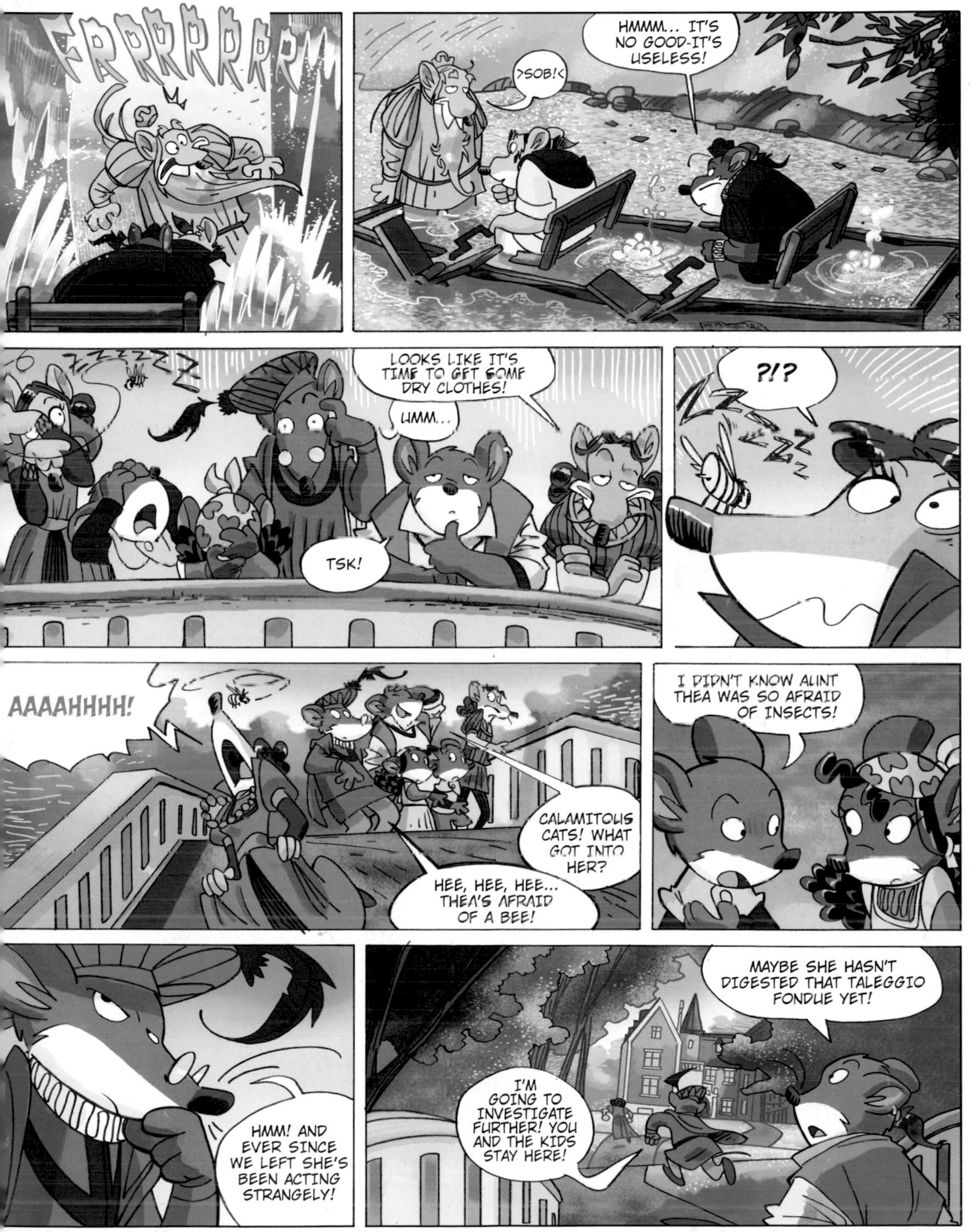
FRRRRRRRM
>SOB!<
HMMM... IT'S NO GOOD-IT'S USELESS!
LOOKS LIKE IT'S TIME TO GET SOME DRY CLOTHES!
UMM...
TSK!
?!?
AAAAHHHH!
CALAMITOUS CATS! WHAT GOT INTO HER?
HEE, HEE, HEE... THEA'S AFRAID OF A BEE!
I DIDN'T KNOW AUNT THEA WAS SO AFRAID OF INSECTS!
HMM! AND EVER SINCE WE LEFT SHE'S BEEN ACTING STRANGELY!
MAYBE SHE HASN'T DIGESTED THAT TALEGGIO FONDUE YET!
I'M GOING TO INVESTIGATE FURTHER! YOU AND THE KIDS STAY HERE!

WHO KNOWS WHERE THEA IS...? SHE'S NOT IN HER ROOM...

THE DOOR TO LEONARDO'S STUDIO IS OPEN! IS SHE HERE?

MOLDY MOZZARELLA!

YOUR MAJESTY, ARE YOU OKAY?

OOOOHHH... WH-WH-WHERE AM I? WHAT HAPPENED TO ME?

CRUMBLING CAMEMBERT! NOW I REMEMBER!

I HEARD A RUSTLING BEHIND ME AND THEN... SOMEONE HIT ME ON THE **HEAD!**

THERE'S A CANDELABRA ON THE FLOOR! IT COULD HAVE BEEN USED TO HIT YOU!

HIT ME? THE KING OF FRANCE? WHAT AN OUTRAGE! GUARDS! **GUARDSSSSSSSSS!**

WHAT A HUGE VOICE! HE'S LIKE GRANDPA TANK!

YIKES! I NEARLY FELL! BUT... BUT... WHAT'S THIS?

A PINK NECKLACE? WHERE DID I JUST SEE IT...?

OH, NO! NOW I REMEMBER WHERE I SAW IT...

MAJESTY... WHAT HAPPENED? WAS THAT YOU *SCREAMING?*

A STRANGER GOT INTO THE STUDIO AND HIT ME ON THE HEAD WITH A CANDELABRA!

BY THE PERSPECTIVE PAINTINGS OF GIOTTO!

BETTER CHECK TO SEE IF ANYTHING WAS STOLEN!

WHY ARE YOU STARING AT ME? IS SOMETHING WRONG?

NO... NO... NOTH-ING...

AFTER A QUICK INSPECTION...

EVERYTHING'S HERE, EXCEPT FOR SOME DRAWINGS OF MACHINES.

IF THE THIEF HOPES TO GET AWAY WITH IT, HE'S MAKING A BIG MISTAKE!

I'LL ORDER THE ROYAL GUARDS TO SEARCH THE CASTLES AND THE VILLAGE, HOUSE BY HOUSE!

BONZETON AND I WILL JOIN THE SEARCH, YOUR MAJESTY!

MY FRIENDS AND I WILL, TOO!

NOW, THAT SOUNDS LIKE WORK...

ALL RIGHT, BUT FIRST LET'S CHECK YOUR ROOMS, TOO!

AFTER SEARCHING ALL THE ROOMS WITH NO RESULTS...

WE ALSO LOOKED FOR THE THIEF THROUGH THE STREETS OF AMBOISE...

36

THAT SAME EVENING, AT THE CASTLE...

NOTHING! WE DIDN'T EVEN FIND A **CLUE!**

DON'T WORRY, STILTONEAUX, YOU DID WHAT YOU COULD!

WELCOME BACK, CATARD! DO YOU HAVE ANY **NEWS?**

WE CHECKED THE WOODS, BUT WE DIDN'T FIND ANYTHING!

AND WHERE DID BONZETON WIND UP? DIDN'T YOU GO TOGETHER TO LOOK FOR THE THIEF?

HE AND I GOT SEPARATED. WHO KNOWS WHERE HE WOUND UP?!

THEN WE'LL HAVE TO ORGANIZE A TEAM TO GO SEARCH FOR HIM!

NOT AT ALL! A LITTLE RAIN WILL CLEAR HIS HEAD!

WELL, THAT'S SETTLED! LET'S GO EAT DINNER!

WE HAD DINNER IN SILENCE AND ALMOST NO ONE HAD ANY APPETITE... EXCEPT TRAP!

THEA WAS REALLY WEIRD TODAY...

EVERYTHING'S GOING ACCORDING TO PLAN!

157,563 + 541,027 = 698,590

YUM! THIS CHEESE IS **DELICIOUS!**

THEN WE SET OFF FOR OUR ROOMS...

THERE'S SOMETHING FUNNY ABOUT THIS THEFT!

DO YOU STILL THINK THAT LEONARDO'S TWO ASSISTANTS ARE THE CATS IN DISGUISE?

I DON'T KNOW BUT I'M VERY **SUSPICIOUS!**

YET BATTISTA, CATARD AND BONZETON WERE AT THE CHANNEL WITH US!

RIGHT... AND BESIDES, THEY STOLE ALMOST NOTHING!

THAT'S EXACTLY WHAT I CAN'T EXPLAIN!

IT'S TIME TO GO TO SLEEP. MAYBE WE'LL GET SOME IDEAS WHILE WE DREAM!

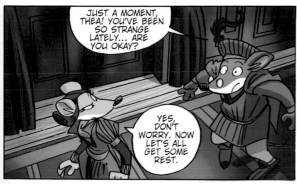
JUST A MOMENT, THEA! YOU'VE BEEN SO STRANGE LATELY... ARE YOU OKAY?

YES, DON'T WORRY. NOW LET'S ALL GET SOME REST.

HMM... OKAY... Goodnight!

GOOD-NIGHT!

'NIGHT!

THREE HOURS LATER...

COUSIN, WOULD YOU STOP WEARING OUT THE FLOOR WITH YOUR PACING?

SORRY.... I'M TOO WORRIED TO SLEEP!

YOU'RE AFRAID YOU WON'T BE ABLE TO STOP THE *PIRATE CATS*?

TO TELL YOU THE TRUTH... I'M *WORRIED* ABOUT THEA!

WORRIED ABOUT THEA?!? WHY?

THIS MORNING, IN LEONARDO'S STUDIO, I FOUND HER NECKLACE ON THE FLOOR!

AND WHAT WAS IT DOING THERE?

THAT'S WHAT I KEEP ASKING MYSELF!

DO YOU SUSPECT THAT SHE STOLE THE DRAWINGS?

NO, BUT... LATELY SHE'S BEEN ACTING **STRANGELY!**

IN MY OPINION, YOU'RE TIRED AND **EXAGGERATING!**

MAYBE SHE ENTERED THE STUDIO, SAW THE KING ON THE GROUND, AND BECAUSE SHE WAS AFRAID SHE'D BE BLAMED FOR THE THEFT, RAN AWAY INSTEAD OF SOUNDING THE ALARM!

THAT'S NOT HOW THEA WOULD ACT! AND HOW DO YOU EXPLAIN THE NECKLACE ON THE FLOOR?

I WOULDN'T KNOW... DID YOU ASK HER?

I TRIED TO, BUT BETWEEN ONE THING AND ANOTHER...

>HMPH< I GET IT! IF I WANT TO SLEEP, I'LL HAVE TO GO WITH YOU TO GET HER TO CLEAR THINGS UP!

A FEW MINUTES LATER...

WE HAVE TO BE QUIET. I DON'T WANT TO WAKE UP THE WHOLE CASTLE!

?!?

BUT... WHAT'S THEA DOING?

MAYBE SHE WANTS A SNACK! LET'S FOLLOW HER!

SHE'S KNOCKING ON THE DOOR OF CATARD AND BONZETON'S ROOM!

NOK NOK

I DON'T UNDER-STAND... WHAT'S GOING ON? LOOK, TRAP, COMING OUT OF THE ROOM IS...

...CATARDONE! AND WHY IS THEA WITH HIM? THEY'VE STOPPED IN FRONT OF LEONARDO'S ROOM!

THEY'RE GOING IN!

WHY IS THEA FOL-LOWING HIM? AND WHAT ARE THEY LOOKING FOR?

MAYBE THE KEY TO THE KITCHEN, FOR A SNACK!

NOW'S THE TIME FOR JOKING AROUND!

COME ON... LET'S GO IN, TOO!

UMM... MAY I COME IN?

BUT THERE'S NO ONE HERE!

THE WINDOW! IT'S WIDE OPEN!

41

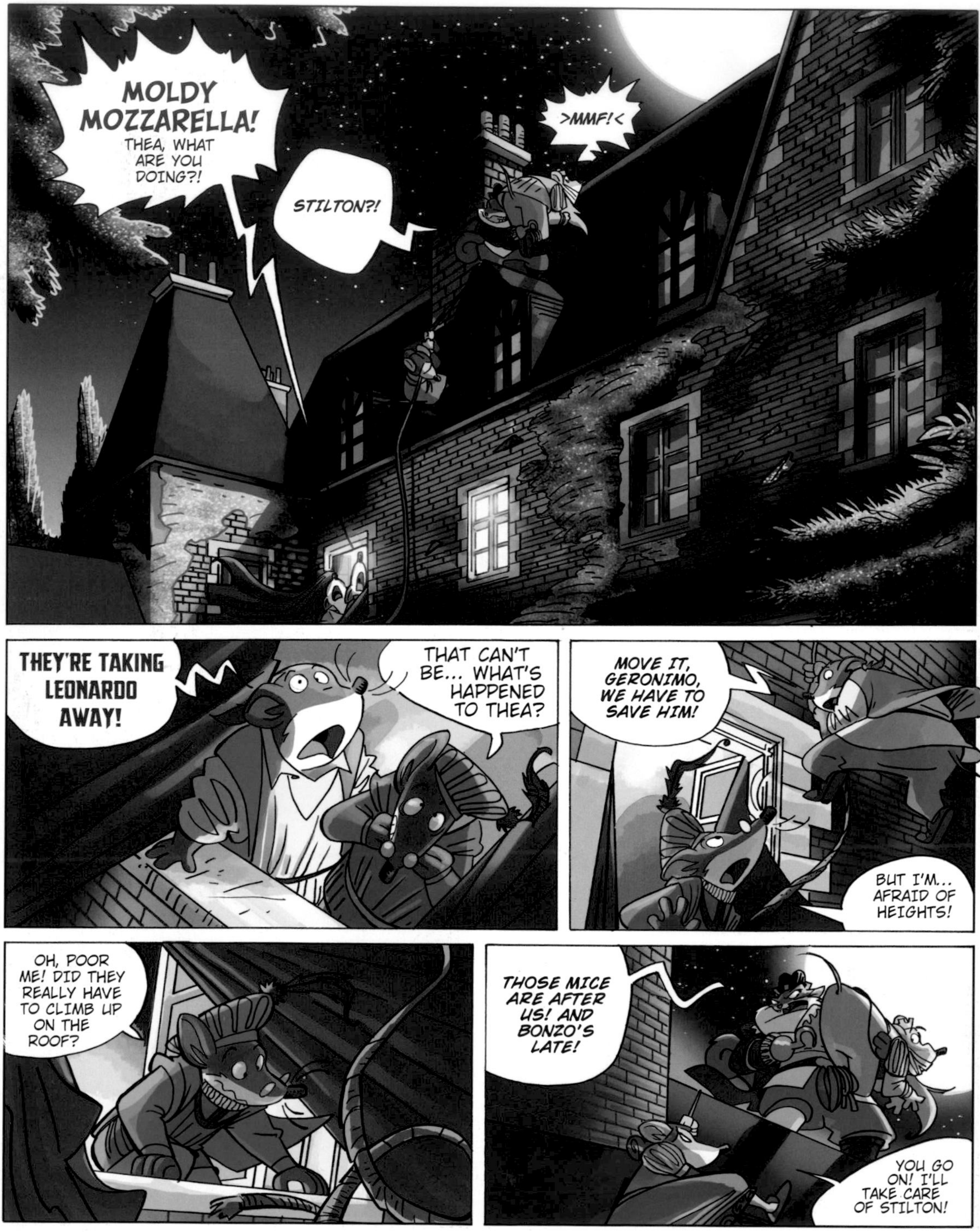
MOLDY MOZZARELLA! THEA, WHAT ARE YOU DOING?!
STILTON?!
>MMF!<
THEY'RE TAKING LEONARDO AWAY!
THAT CAN'T BE... WHAT'S HAPPENED TO THEA?
MOVE IT, GERONIMO, WE HAVE TO SAVE HIM!
BUT I'M... AFRAID OF HEIGHTS!
OH, POOR ME! DID THEY REALLY HAVE TO CLIMB UP ON THE ROOF?
THOSE MICE ARE AFTER US! AND BONZO'S LATE!
YOU GO ON! I'LL TAKE CARE OF STILTON!

STOP RIGHT THERE!

THEA, WHAT'S GOTTEN INTO YOU?

THEA?

>TSK<... YOU SHOULD'VE KNOWN I'M NOT YOUR SISTER!

SURPRISE!

TERSILLA!

WH-WH-WHAT DID YOU DO WITH THEA?

YOUR SISTER'S IN NEW MOUSE CITY! I GAGGED HER AND PUT HER TO SLEEP RIGHT BEFORE YOU ARRIVED!

BUT... I DON'T UNDERSTAND... WHY DID YOU TAKE HER PLACE?

OBVIOUSLY, TO DISCOVER HOW YOU FIND OUT ABOUT OUR TIME TRAVELS--AND TO KEEP YOU FROM ALWAYS MAKING OUR PLANS GO UP IN SMOKE!

NOW I KNOW ALL ABOUT PROFESSOR VOLT AND HIS TEMPOGRAPH!

YOU CRUMMY CAT! I'M GOING TO MAKE YOU PAY FOR THIS!

SO IT WAS YOU WHO STOLE THE DRAWINGS FROM LEONARDO'S STUDIO AND HIT THE KING!

EXACTLY! I WANTED TO THROW OFF YOUR SUSPICIONS AND MAKE YOU THINK THAT THE CATS HAD COME FROM OUTSIDE! THE BEE GAVE ME AN EXCUSE TO LEAVE AND GO BACK TO THE CASTLE...

"THE INVESTIGATION WOULD HAVE CONTINUED AND WE PIRATE CATS WOULD HAVE BEEN ABLE TO OPERATE WITHOUT BEING DISTURBED... AND KIDNAP LEONARDO!"

"AS FOR THE KING, I DIDN'T EXPECT TO MEET HIM. BUT TAKING CARE OF HIM WAS CHILD'S PLAY!"

I BET YOU BROKE THE **NECKLACE** WHEN YOU HIT HIM, AND THAT'S WHY IT WAS ON THE FLOOR!

HUH? IT LOOKS LIKE I MADE A MISTAKE! I WAS IN SUCH A HURRY THAT I DIDN'T EVEN NOTICE I'D LOST IT!

BUT WHY DID YOU WANT TO **KIDNAP** LEONARDO?

TO DECODE THE TEXT ON THIS PARCHMENT! IT MUST HAVE INSTRUCTIONS FOR FINDING A CAT-TAS-TIC TREASURE!

TIME FOR US TO SAY GOODBYE, STILTON: BUNZO'S HERE WITH THE CATJET!

HE PRETENDED TO GET LOST IN THE WOODS SO HE COULD GO GET THE TIME MACHINE!

QUICK, GERONIMO... YOU'VE GOT TO DO SOMETHING!

ME? WHAT?

WHATEVER!

>GULP!<

I'M SLIIIIDING!

SQUEEEEEEEEE

45

MEEOWWW!

THE PARCHMENT! NOOOO!

KLOP!

A THOUSAND TUMBLING TABBY CATS!

>MMPH!<

GRRR... I'M GOING MAKE YOU PAY FOR THAT, YOU LOUSY RAT!

SQUEAK!

DID YOU HEAR THAT RUCKUS, TOO?

IT SOUNDS LIKE IT CAME FROM THE ROOF!

HAVE THE THIEVES RETURNED? WE MUST SOUND THE ALARM!

ATTENTION! THE THIEVES HAVE COME BACK TO THE CASTLE OF CLOUX!

THE THIEVES ARE AT THE CASTLE!

?!?

TERSILLA, CATARDONE, HURRY UP! THE SOLDIERS ARE COMING!

LET'S GET OUT OF HERE, DADDY DEAR! NOW!

BUT... BUT... AND LEAVE THE PARCHMENT AND LEONARDO?

WOULD YOU RATHER SPEND THE REST OF YOUR DAYS IN PRISON?

UM... NO! EMPHATICALLY ... NO!

YOU WON AGAIN, STILTON! BUT WE'LL MEET AGAIN!

AT LEAST THIS TIME IT'S NOT MY FAULT THAT THE PLAN WAS RUINED!

>GULP!< I SINCERELY HOPE NOT!

SO, HERE WE WERE AT THE END OF OUR ADVENTURE. AFTER HAVING FOILED THE CATS' PLAN AND RECOVERING THE STOLEN DRAWINGS, WE TOLD LEONARDO THE WHOLE TRUTH!

WHEN WE TOLD HIM ABOUT THE TIME MACHINE, HE DIDN'T SEEM SURPRISED!

I WAS SURE THERE'D BE TIME TRAVEL SOONER OR LATER!

BUT I WON'T TELL ANYONE ANYTHING ABOUT IT, SO THAT HISTORY DOESN'T CHANGE!

THANK YOU, YOU'RE A TRUE *gentlemouse!*

BETTER YET, I'D BE CURIOUS TO SEE THE PARCHMENT!

HERE IT IS! IT FELL FROM THE *ROOF!*

ROLLICKING RATS! IT'S... THE RECIPE FOR RIBOLLITA!

RIBOLLITA?!?

SJCPMMJUB

IT MUST BE A JOKE FROM SOME PRANKSTER COOK! IT'S WRITTEN IN A CODE WHERE EACH LETTER IN A WORD IS WRITTEN DOWN BY USING THE NEXT LETTER IN THE ALPHABET! LOOK, HERE'S THE CODE: R=S, I=J, B=C, O=P, L=M, L=M, I=J, T=U, A=B!

THOSE CATS WENT TO ALL THAT TROUBLE JUST FOR A BOWL OF *SOUP?*

HA, HA, HA!

IT SEEMS LIKE A VERY GOOD REASON TO ME!

RIBOLLITA

IS A TYPICAL TUSCAN SOUP. ITS INGREDIENTS ARE KALE, BEETS, SAVOY CABBAGE, LEEKS, ONIONS, CELERY, POTATOES, CARROTS, ZUCCHINI, TOMATOES, CANNELLINI BEANS, EXTRA-VIRGIN OLIVE OIL, SALT, PEPPER, AND BREAD. BOIL THE BEANS AND SAUTÉ THE ONIONS AND OTHER CHOPPED VEGETABLES IN THE OLIVE OIL. ADD THE BEANS, HALF OF WHICH HAVE BEEN PUT THROUGH A SIEVE AND THE OTHER HALF LEFT WHOLE. COOK OVER A SLOW FIRE FOR AROUND TWO HOURS. ADD THE SLICED BREAD, SALT, AND PEPPER AND SERVE WITH A DROP OF OLIVE OIL.

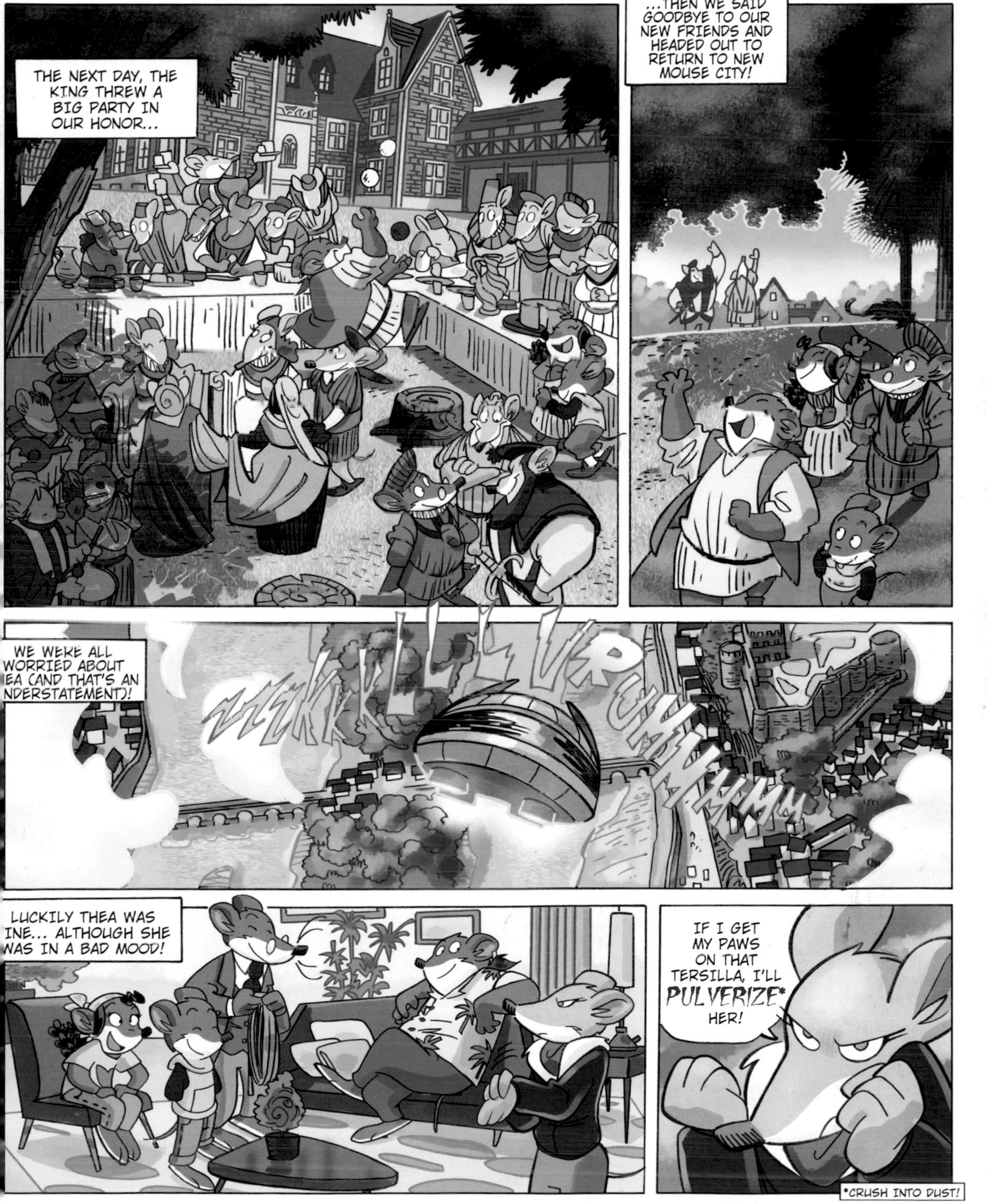
THE NEXT DAY, THE KING THREW A BIG PARTY IN OUR HONOR...
...THEN WE SAID GOODBYE TO OUR NEW FRIENDS AND HEADED OUT TO RETURN TO NEW MOUSE CITY!
WE WERE ALL WORRIED ABOUT EA (AND THAT'S AN NDERSTATEMENT)!
ZZZKKK!!! VRUMMMMMMM
LUCKILY THEA WAS INE... ALTHOUGH SHE WAS IN A BAD MOOD!
IF I GET MY PAWS ON THAT TERSILLA, I'LL PULVERIZE* HER!
*CRUSH INTO DUST!

A LITTLE LATER, WE'D MADE OUR WAY BACK TO PROFESSOR VOLT'S LAB, AND WE TOLD HIM THE WHOLE STORY...

I'M HAPPY THAT THE MISSION WAS A SUCCESS!

BUT NOW THE PIRATE CATS KNOW ABOUT YOUR LAB AND THE TEMPOGRAPH!

WELL, MY LABORATORY'S ALWAYS ON THE MOVE, SO THOSE CRUMMY CATS WON'T BE ABLE TO LOCATE IT! AND THEY'RE NOT GOING TO BE ABLE TO TRICK THE TEMPOGRAPH!

SO SHALL WE BEGIN OUR CELEBRATION?

>SLURP!< DEFINITELY!

SO, GERONIMO, WHAT KIND OF A BIRD, OR RATHER A RAT, WAS LEONARDO?

HE WAS LIKE YOU IN MANY WAYS, PROFESSOR!

THANKS FOR THE COMPLIMENT! I'VE ALWAYS CONSIDERED LEONARDO TO BE ONE OF MY TEACHERS! AND I THINK I'VE FOLLOWED HIS TEACHING TO GOOD EFFECT.

>TSK<... FROM THE LOOK OF THIS DRAWING, I WOULDN'T EXACTLY SAY SO!

>GULP!<

MY DEAR RODENT FRIENDS, FAREWELL UNTIL THE NEXT ADVENTURE... ANOTHER WHISKERFUL OF AN ADVENTURE, WRITTEN BY STILTON...

Geronimo Stilton!

Watch Out For PAPERCUTZ

On my way to the Papercutz offices every day, I usually pick up a newspaper. It's not the Rodent's Gazette, because I don't live in New Mouse City, it's the New York Post. With so much to do at Papercutz, I simply don't have the time to read the far more substantial New York Times or The Wall Street Journal. There are a couple of free newspapers, but they're a bit too skimpy. There's also The New York Daily News, which features the most comics, but the paper has grown quite stodgy over the years. Oh, wait—I forgot to introduce myself again! I'm Salicrup, *Jim Salicrup*, and I'm the Editor-in-Chief of Papercutz, the all-ages graphic novel publisher.

I'm curious—which is why I read a newspaper every day— do you read a daily newspaper? And if so, is it the printed edition or an online or digital version? Once upon a time almost everyone read a newspaper, but these days not so much. The question is—what happened? The reason I'm asking the question here in the pages of GERONIMO STILTON is that Geronimo is a newspaper editor. So many famous comicbook characters work in the newspaper field— Clark Kent, who is a mild-mannered reporter for The Daily Planet, a great metropolitan newspaper, and Peter Parker is a freelance photographer for The Daily Bugle. Newspapers have been the settings for such characters because it places the heroes right where the action is—reporters travel the world covering all the major news stories of the day! But sadly, newspapers are not doing so well these days. Circulation is heading down, not up, as many people turn to either television or the Internet for their news.

So, I'm asking you—yes, you—what do you think about all this? If you do read newspapers, please tell us why, and what you enjoy most. If you don't, we'd like to know why—are they too boring? Not covering things that interest you? Are they too hard to understand? What would you do, if you were a newspaper editor? How would you change the newspaper to make it appeal more to younger people? Do you think newspapers should go the way of the dinosaurs and just quietly fade into the past? Or do you think there's something newspapers could do that could make them part of your daily routine? Please email your answers to me at salicrup@papercutz.com or send it through the mail to Jim Salicrup, PAPERCUTZ, 40 Exchange Place, Suite 1308, New York, NY 10005. Oh, and be sure to also let me know what you think of our GERONIMO STILTON graphic novels! Even if you don't care about newspapers—we want to know what you think about Geronimo!

Also, don't forget to visit www.papercutz.com! There's a lot of new and exciting Papercutz graphic novels heading your way soon, and I'm sure you won't want to miss it! Everything from HARRY POTTY to THE SMURFS! And don't miss GERONIMO STILTON Graphic Novel #7 "Dinosaurs in Action"! There's a short preview starting on the very next page...

So, until next time, try not to go back in time for any selfish or devious reasons, Geronimo already has his hands full saving the future, by protecting the past, without you starting trouble!

Thanks, *Jim*

AS WE'D AGREED, WE SPLIT UP...

HEY, GERONIMO, LOOK OUT FOR THAT BRANCH!

WHAT BRANCH?

THAT BRANCH!

OUCH!

IF YOU ONLY THINK ABOUT FOLLOWING THE TRACKS AND ALWAYS KEEP YOUR EYES GLUED TO THE GROUND...

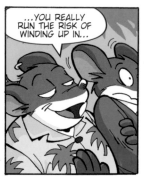

...YOU REALLY RUN THE RISK OF WINDING UP IN...

...HOT WATER!

HELP!

OW, OW! THAT HURT!

OUCH!

THUMP

WHOMP

THIS PIT SHOULDN'T BE HERE! SOMEONE COULD FALL IN AND BRUISE THEIR TAILBONE!

JUST LIKE WE DID...

>GULP!< I HOPE I'M WRONG, BUT THIS DOESN'T SEEM TO BE A NORMAL PIT!

?!?

LOOK! WE FELL RIGHT INTO THE TRACK OF A DINOSAUR!

>GULP!< YOU'RE RIGHT... IT'S REALLY HUGE!

IT'S GOT TO BE A TITANOSAUR! I READ SOMEWHERE THAT IT'S ONE OF THE BIGGEST TERRESTRIAL DINOSAURS THAT EVER EXISTED!

THE TITANOSAUR

WAS A HERBIVOROUS DINOSAUR THAT LIVED IN THE CRETACEOUS PERIOD. IT COULD REACH A LENGTH OF 49 FEET AND A WEIGHT OF 20 TONS. ITS ELONGATED, FLEXIBLE NECK ENDED IN A TINY HEAD AND ITS MASSIVE BODY WAS SUPPORTED BY SQUAT LEGS LIKE THOSE OF AN ELEPHANT. A ROW OF BONY PLATES RAN ALONG ITS BACK.

DON'T GET STRESSED OUT, COUSIN!... MAYBE IT WAS JUST A LIZARD WITH SLIGHTLY SWOLLEN FEET THAT PASSED THROUGH HERE!

LET'S GRAB ONTO THIS BRANCH AND TRY TO GET OUT OF HERE!

BRANCH? ODD, I DIDN'T SEE THAT BEFORE!

GRRRRRRRR

DID YOU SAY SOMETHING, GERONIMO?

UM, NO! I THOUGHT THAT WAS YOUR **STOMACH!**

GRRRRR...

MOLDY MOZZARELLA!

HELP!

GRUNT!

SQUEEEAK!

SBAMM

SCNACK

SQUOOOSH

OUGH!

BLECH! THESE BERRIES I FELL ON ARE STICKY! AND WHAT A SMELL!

DON'T WHINE: WE'RE LUCKY! THAT BEAST IS MORE INTERESTED IN THE FRESH LEAVES THAN IN US!

TRICERATOPS
THE NAME OF THIS DINOSAUR MEANS "THREE-HORNED FACE." AS A MATTER OF FACT, IT TYPICALLY HAD TWO LONG HORNS LOCATED ABOVE ITS EYES--WHICH COULD REACH THE LENGTH OF OVER THREE FEET AND A SHORTER HORN ON TOP OF ITS NOSE. IT ALSO HAD A BONY COLLAR THAT CIRCLED ITS WHOLE NECK AND PROTECTED IT FROM ATTACKS BY OTHER DINOSAURS. TRICERATOPS WAS AN HERBIVORE, AND COULD REACH A LENGTH OF OVER 26 FEET AND A WEIGHT OF 7-8 TONS.

Don't miss GERONIMO STILTON Graphic Novel #7 – "Dinosaurs in Action"!

The first three Geronimo Stilton Graphic Novels collected in one box...

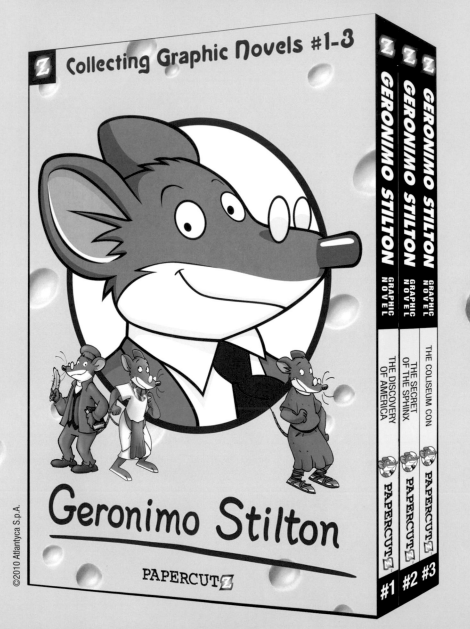

Collecting Graphic Novels #1-3

Geronimo Stilton

PAPERCUTZ

©2010 Atlantyca S.p.A.

GERONIMO STILTON GRAPHIC NOVEL THE DISCOVERY OF AMERICA PAPERCUTZ #1

GERONIMO STILTON GRAPHIC NOVEL THE SECRET OF THE SPHINX PAPERCUTZ #2

GERONIMO STILTON GRAPHIC NOVEL THE COLISEUM CON PAPERCUTZ #3

Available at booksellers everywhere.

THE PIRATE CATS TRAVEL TO THE PAST ON THE CATJET SO THAT THEY CAN CHANGE HISTORY AND BECOME RICH AND FAMOUS. BUT GERONIMO AND THE STILTON FAMILY ALWAYS MANAGE TO UNMASK THEM!